Disney

Family Story Collection

— ⌘ —

Never Stop
Believing

W9-DHF-413

STORIES ABOUT HOPE

— ⌘ —

Book Nine

Collection copyright © 2005 Disney Enterprises, Inc.

All rights reserved. No part of this book may be reproduced or
transmitted in any form or by any means, electronic or mechanical,
including photocopying, recording, or by any information storage
and retrieval system, without written permission from the publisher.
For information address Disney Press,
114 Fifth Avenue, New York, New York 10011-5690.

Printed in China
First Edition
1 3 5 7 9 10 8 6 4 2

ISBN 0-7868-3533-8

For more Disney Press fun, visit www.disneybooks.com

Book Nine

Never Stop Believing

STORIES ABOUT HOPE

Introduction

Children are born believing in the wonder of the world around them. To a child's eyes, a rainbow, the stars at night, a caterpillar turning into a butterfly can be as magical as good fairies and talking puppets. As they grow older, children may feel they have outgrown some of this amazement, but there are always limitless possibilities open to them. If youngsters believe hard enough, their dreams may come true.

In "A Silver Lining," Princess Aurora is given many gifts when she is born, but the one that matters the most is the gift of hope. It will see her through dark times and lead to a lifetime of happiness. In "Geppetto's Wish," Pinocchio's belief is so strong that, miraculously, his wish is granted and he comes to life.

A Silver Lining

from *Sleeping Beauty*

When all seems lost, a little hope makes a big difference.

It was a joyous day for King Stefan and the Queen. They had proclaimed a great holiday throughout the kingdom so that everyone might come to the castle to honor their firstborn child, Princess Aurora.

Among the many guests were the three
good fairies: Flora, Fauna, and Merryweather.

"The little darling," cooed Merryweather
as the fairies peeked inside Aurora's cradle.
The fairies would bestow gifts upon the
princess, but each could give one, and
only one.

Flora was the first to step up to the cradle. She waved her wand over the child, saying, "Little princess, my gift shall be the gift of beauty."

Next, Fauna approached the cradle. "My gift shall be the gift of song," she said.

Last but not least, it was Merryweather's turn. "Sweet princess, my gift shall be the—"

Just then, a wicked wind blew through the castle. Huge flames engulfed the great hall. Out of the fire stepped the evil fairy, Maleficent.

Maleficent looked around at the guests. "King Stefan," she said snidely, "I really felt quite distressed at not receiving an invitation."

"You weren't wanted," replied Merryweather, red-faced and angry.

Maleficent pretended to be embarrassed. "Well, in that case, I'll be on my way," she said. But before she left, Maleficent announced that she, too, had a gift to give the child.

"The princess shall indeed grow

in grace and beauty, beloved by all who know her," Maleficent began. "But on her sixteenth birthday, she shall prick her finger on the spindle of a spinning wheel . . . and die!"

King Stefan ordered his guards to seize Maleficent. But in a flash of smoke, she was gone.

King Stefan and the Queen were beside themselves with grief. But Flora reassured them, "Don't despair, Your Majesties. Merryweather still has her gift to give."

"Can she undo this awful curse?" King Stefan asked.

"Oh, no, Sire," Merryweather said sadly.

"Maleficent's powers are far too great," added Flora.

"But she can help," said Fauna. She turned to Merryweather. "Just do your best, dear."

Merryweather waved her wand, creating an image of a sleeping sixteen-year-old princess. "Sweet princess," she began, "if through this wicked witch's trick, a spindle should your finger prick, a ray of hope there still may be in this gift

I give to thee. Not in death, but in sleep the fateful prophecy you'll keep, and from this slumber you shall wake, when True Love's Kiss the spell shall break."

And so it was that Merryweather's gift was not only a gift to Aurora but to King Stefan, the Queen, and the entire kingdom. It was the gift of hope—hope that Maleficent's evil spell would someday be broken.

Geppetto's Wish

from *Pinocchio*

Make a wish—it just may come true.

Long ago, on a clear night in a quaint little village, a kind, old wood-carver named Geppetto was working in his workshop. He was putting the finishing touches on his newest handmade puppet.

"That makes a big difference!" Geppetto exclaimed as he painted a smile on the puppet's wooden face. "Now, I have just the name for you," he said. "Pinocchio!"

Geppetto turned on a music box and began to dance the puppet around his shop, introducing Pinocchio to his cat, Figaro, and his fish, Cleo. They all sang and danced until—*cuckoo, cuckoo*—Geppetto's many clocks struck the late hour.

Then Geppetto climbed into bed and, as Figaro settled down to sleep next to him, the wood-carver stared across the room at Pinocchio. "He almost looks alive!" Geppetto said to Figaro. "Wouldn't it be nice if he were a real boy?"

Geppetto then realized he had forgotten to open the window as he did every night at bedtime. Figaro, being closer, got up and opened it. "Oh, Figaro, look!" Geppetto exclaimed, pointing to a bright star in the sky. "The wishing star!"

In an instant, Geppetto was kneeling before the open window, making a wish on the brilliant star. Then, with his wish made, Geppetto confided to his cat, "I wished that my little Pinocchio might be a real boy!" He climbed back into bed, saying to himself,

"Just think. A real boy . . . a real boy . . ."

Soon, both Geppetto and Figaro were sleeping soundly—so soundly that they did not awaken when an amazing thing happened. In the stillness of the night, a bright light—as bright as a wishing star— traveled through the open window and into the room.

The light took the shape of a beautiful fairy—the Blue Fairy. She stood over the sleeping Geppetto and said, "You deserve to have your wish come true!" Silently, the Blue Fairy crossed the room, touched her wand to Pinocchio's head, and said, "Little puppet made of pine, wake! The gift of life is thine."

At that, a bright light emanated from the Blue Fairy's wand. When it faded, Pinocchio's eyes blinked, and he raised his hands to rub them together.

"I can move!" Pinocchio exclaimed. He covered his mouth, surprised at the words that had come out. "I can talk!" he added with delight.

"Yes, Pinocchio," said the Blue Fairy. "I have given you life!" She advised Pinocchio to be good and to listen to his conscience before she faded away like a dream and was gone.

A short time later, Pinocchio, still getting used to his legs, tripped over some paint pots. The noise awoke Geppetto, who was amazed to find that his little wooden puppet was alive! At first, Geppetto was convinced that he was dreaming. But the proof was right in front of him. Before long, Geppetto began to believe his good fortune.

"It's—it's—my wish—" he said joyfully as
he picked up Pinocchio. "It's come true!"